Denver Public Library

IN MEMORY OF:

Bess E. Miller

1972

P. C. Asbjørnsen and J. E. Moe

THE
THREE
BILLY
GOATS
GRUFF

Pictures by

MARCIA BROWN

Harcourt, Brace & World, Inc.

New York

To *Anne Carroll Moore and the Troll*

Taken from the translation of G. W. Dasent

© *1957 by Marcia Brown*

Library of Congress catalog card number: 57-5265

Printed in the United States of America

LMNOPQR

ONCE on a time there were three billy goats
who were to go up to the hillside to make themselves
fat, and the name of all three was "Gruff."

On the way up was a bridge over a river they had to cross, and under the bridge lived a great ugly troll with eyes as big as saucers and a nose as long as a poker.

So first of all came the youngest
Billy Goat Gruff to cross the bridge.
"Trip, trap! trip, trap!" went the bridge.

"*Who's that tripping over my bridge?*" roared the troll.
"Oh, it is only I, the tiniest Billy
Goat Gruff, and I'm going up
to the hillside to make myself fat,"
said the billy goat with such a small voice.
"*Now, I'm coming to gobble you up!*" said the troll.

"Oh, no! pray don't take me. I'm too little, that I am," said the billy goat. "Wait a bit till the second Billy Goat Gruff comes. He's much bigger." "Well! be off with you," said the troll.

A little while after came the second
Billy Goat Gruff to cross the bridge.
"Trip, trap! trip, trap! trip, trap!"
went the bridge.

"Who's that tripping over my bridge?" roared the troll.
"Oh, it's the second Billy Goat Gruff,
and I'm going up to the hillside to
make myself fat," said the billy goat,
and his voice was not so small.

"Now, I'm coming to gobble you up!" said the troll.

"Oh, no! don't take me. Wait a little till the big Billy Goat Gruff comes. He's much bigger." "Very well! Be off with you," said the troll.

Just then, up came the big Billy Goat Gruff.
"T-r-i-p, t-r-a-p! t-r-i-p, t-r-a-p!
t-r-i-p, t-r-a-p!" went the bridge, for the
billy goat was so heavy that the bridge
creaked and groaned under him.
"*Who's that tramping over my bridge?*" roared the troll.

"It's I! the
BIG BILLY GOAT
GRUFF!"
said the billy goat, who had an
ugly hoarse voice of his own.

"*Now, I'm coming to gobble you up!*" roared the troll.

"Well, come along! I've got two spears,
And I'll poke your eyeballs out at your ears.
I've got besides two great big stones,
And I'll crush you to bits, body and bones."

That was what the billy goat said;
and so he flew at the troll, and
poked his eyes out with his horns,
and crushed him to bits, body and
bones, and tossed him into the river.

Then he went up to the hillside.

There the billy goats got so fat they were
scarce able to walk again; and if the fat hasn't
fallen off them, why they're still fat; and so—
"Snip, snap, snout.
This tale's told out."